I'm Not Wearing That!

Story by Jane Clarke
Pictures by David Mostyn

...dingles & company

Yorik the Yellow always wore yellow,

Olaf the Blue always wore blue,

and Erika the Red always wore red.

Then, one day Mrs. Viking went off to build a boat and left Mr. Viking in charge.

"Make sure they wear the right color outfits, dear," she told him. "And don't forget to do the washing!"

"I'll do my best," said Dad.

3

On Monday, Dad couldn't find one of Erika's red boots.

"Erika," he said, "you will have to wear one of Olaf's spare boots today."

"I'm not wearing that," said Erika. "It's blue. I always wear red. Red is cool. Red is the color of blood! Blue is the color of little bluebirds."

"Blue is the color of giant blue whales!" said Dad.

"Cool!" said Erika. She put on the blue boot.

5

On Tuesday, Dad couldn't find Erika's pants.

"Erika," he said. "You will have to wear a spare pair of Yorik's pants today."

"I'm not wearing those," said Erika. 'They are yellow. I always wear red. Red is the color of the sunset! Yellow is the color of little buttercups."

"Yellow is the color of pirate gold!" said Dad.

"Gold! That's cool!" said Erika. So she put on Yorik's yellow pants.

Gold!

On Wednesday, Dad washed Erika's red shirt with Yorik's yellow cape.

"Wow!" said Dad. "They have both changed color. The red and the yellow have mixed together."

Wow!

"I'm not wearing that shirt," said Erika.
"It's orange. Our little kitten is orange."
"Volcanoes are orange!" said Dad.
"Wow! Orange!" said Erika. She put the
orange shirt on.

Wow! Orange!

9

On Wednesday night, Dad left Erika's shield out all night and it became all moldy and green.

"I'm not wearing that," said Erika on Thursday. "It looks green. Grass is green."

"So is slimy eel soup!" said Dad.

"Cool" said Erika. "Slime green is cool!" And she put on the green shield.

Cool!

On Friday, Dad washed Erika's red cape with Olaf's blue pants.

"Ooooooops!" said Dad. "The colors got all mixed up again."

"I'm not wearing that," said Erika. "It's purple, like Mom's old necklace."

"Purple is the color of a wild and stormy night at sea!" said Dad.
"Cool! Stormy purple!" said Erika, putting on the purple cape.

On Saturday, Dad boiled the white sheets along with Erika's red helmet.
"Oh dear! Not again!" he groaned.

"I'm not wearing that!" said Erika. "It's pink! Only girls wear pink!"

"You are a girl!" said Dad.

"I'm a Viking," said Erika. "Vikings don't wear pink."

"But pink is the color of a hungry wolf's tongue!" said Dad.

"That's cool!" said Erika, and she put on the pink helmet.

That's cool!

On Sunday, Mom came home. She gave them all a hug and a kiss.

16

"I'll sort it out, dear," said Mom, getting out her hammer and chisel.

"We'll keep the other colors in case we have any more children!" she said, gathering up all the clothes.

She carved the words RED, YELLOW, PINK, GREEN, BLUE, ORANGE, and PURPLE on seven different boxes.

Then, on Monday, Mom put out Erika's outfit for her to wear.

Here you are, Erika.

"I'm not wearing that outfit," said Erika.
"All those things are red! I always wear lots of
different colors!"

I'm **not** wearing **that** outfit!

21

Erika opened all the boxes and took out
one green boot,
    one purple boot,
        a pair of pink pants,
        a red shirt,
            a yellow helmet,

. . . a blue shield,
and an orange cape.

"But Erika," said Mom. "Your name is Erika the Red!"

"Not anymore!" said Erika. She put on her new outfit. "From now on, I'm Erika the Rainbow."

I'm Erica the Rainbow.

Cool!

We want to be rainbows, too!

And from that day on Erika the Rainbow, Yorik the Rainbow, and Olaf the Rainbow always wore lots of colors. So life was a whole lot easier for Mr. Viking when he was left in charge.